SCENES FROM THE UNDERGROUND

Scenes from the Underground

Gabriel Cholette

With Illustrations by Jacob Pyne

Translated by Elina Taillon

ARACHNIDE

First published as *Les carnets de l'underground* in 2021 by Triptyque
First published in English in 2022 by House of Anansi Press Inc.
www.houseofanansi.com

House of Anansi Press is committed to protecting our natural environment. This book is made of material from well-managed FSC®-certified forests, recycled materials, and other controlled sources.

House of Anansi Press is a Global Certified Accessible™ (GCA by Benetech) publisher. The ebook version of this book meets stringent accessibility standards and is available to students and readers with print disabilities.

26 25 24 23 22   1 2 3 4 5

Library and Archives Canada Cataloguing in Publication

Title: Scenes from the underground / Gabriel Cholette ; with illustrations by Jacob Pyne ; translated by Elina Taillon.
Other titles: Carnets de l'underground. English
Names: Cholette, Gabriel, author. | Pyne, Jacob, illustrator. | Taillon, Elina, translator.
Description: Translation of: Les carnets de l'underground.
Identifiers: Canadiana (print) 20220224064 | Canadiana (ebook) 20220224218 | ISBN 9781487010751 (softcover) | ISBN 9781487010768 (EPUB)
Subjects: LCSH: Cholette, Gabriel. | LCSH: Gay men—Social life and customs—Biography. | LCSH: Dance parties. | LCGFT: Autobiographies.
Classification: LCC HQ75.8.C56 A3 2022 | DDC 306.76/62092—dc23

Cover illustration by Jacob Pyne

House of Anansi Press respectfully acknowledges that the land on which we operate is the Traditional Territory of many Nations, including the Anishinabeg, the Wendat, and the Haudenosaunee. It is also the Treaty Lands of the Mississaugas of the Credit.

 Canada Council **Conseil des Arts**
for the Arts **du Canada**

 ONTARIO ARTS COUNCIL
CONSEIL DES ARTS DE L'ONTARIO
an Ontario government agency
un organisme du gouvernement de l'Ontario

With the participation of the Government of Canada
Avec la participation du gouvernement du Canada |  Canadä

We acknowledge the financial support of the Government of Canada through the National Translation Program for Book Publishing, an initiative of the Action Plan for Official Languages — 2018–2023: Investing in Our Future, for our translation activities.

Printed and bound in Canada

MIX
Paper from
responsible sources
FSC
www.fsc.org   FSC® C103567

Don't send this to my mother.

LEGEND
Berlin, Germany

Bert puts me up on the edge of the stall to take test photos because the lighting is good. I have just heard for the first time the expression "to make soup": it means to mix the bottom-of-the-pocket drugs of everyone huddled in the club toilet stall, opened MD, ketamine, old dry speed, crushed e pills, to make big lines that will let us forget the past forty-eight hours that have been so difficult.

Two days before the soup, I'm bored at Emma's place; I tell myself I'm not experiencing Berlin fully enough. I message someone on Grindr who looks straight and seems to be propositioning a guy for the first time in his life. Next. I message a dude with lips a little too full for my taste. We exchange photos. Next. Even more bored than before.

I

The first guy replies to let me know he's sitting next to the second. I realize that he's not straight and clearly not undercover in his new homosexual life when he explains that he's at an orgy party and that there are twelve people sucking each other off in the next room.

That's not my sort of thing, but even so I agree to play the game; the dirty talk succeeds just as much at turning me on as it does at making me realize that if I go over there, I'll be, quite frankly, the service hole. I end up telling the boys that I accept their invitation on the condition that no one joins our threesome and that they show me a little respect.

Of course, that doesn't work. A fourth one (not ugly) joins us, the others push on my head to get me on my knees, but, before doing anything, I tell them that this isn't what was agreed on, that I'm not comfortable, and that I want to leave. The three understand right away, we begin a quick little conversation (*what do you do for a living?* they enumerate: *law fashion cinema*) and suddenly they win some points: I find myself a bit seduced.

I think that if we'd talked a little longer, I might have stayed, but it's fine because Florian messaged me when I left and we spent the rest of the day snuggling on a lakeshore.

The next day, I find myself at Buttons with Sophy and Emma, and, going up to the cloakroom, I spot in the distance the "straight" guy trying to avoid my gaze. I manage to dodge his as well, except in the toilets I run right into him, and he explains to me that he felt like crap all day because I'd seemed very uncomfortable the night before. I tell him that it wasn't traumatizing, that I was just sticking to my boundaries. He introduces himself in passing, *Bert*. I hear Bart, like Bart Simpson, and I call him Bart for at least an hour before he finally corrects me.

From that moment on, we were never apart, to the point where the girls spent three hours looking for me, doing the rounds from the dance floor to the toilets by way of the dark rooms, where they thought they saw a guy having a full-on heart attack on the ground but who was just jerking off. All this while Bert had me dancing "robot-style," stuck on the ends of his feet while he controlled my legs and my arms and we fell, thanks to the magic of Berlin, madly in love.

(There really was something magical: Bert was leaving in twelve hours and we didn't want to lose a single second of the time we could spend together.)

I accompanied him to his Neukölln apartment to help him pack while we both cried our hearts out. We Skyped four days later and, trying to look cute, I overturned the wooden table on which I'd set myself up, in the process knocking over the four plants that were there. He didn't seem to find this cute, and he told me, already reluctantly, that I could swing by New York to see him during Fashion Week if I wanted.

The guy lived in Manhattan — the dream — and since I was in love, I decided to take off again as soon as I got back to Montreal, already imagining myself moving to the mythical city that gave rise to *Sex and the City*. My Amigo Express lift was four hours late, but at last I fell into Bert's arms in a Lower East Side park next to which we went to eat fried chicken with one of his model friends, who only ordered coleslaw.

It's rather tragic that I arrived late because that was our only good day together in New York. I spent all the others waiting for him in his apartment with not much to do before he would come home and turn grumpy, and we would bicker without me understanding why.

Even more frustrating: he makes me buy a ticket for an after-party ($50 US because everything is ultra-expensive in New York) but avoids me the whole evening, until I decide to leave without telling him. Struck by misgiving, I come back and tell him that his attitude, it's kind of shit, and he stammers something, introduces me to a tall handsome guy, like really handsome, and we spend all of three seconds together and they find a pretext for abandoning me.

On the verge of tears, I go back to Bert's place, telling myself that he's got to return eventually, but he texts me to announce that he's not coming home: he had an argument with the tall handsome guy, like really too tall, and he lets me know that the guy in question is his boyfriend and they were already dating when we met in Berlin.

Can anyone explain to me what I'm doing in New York waiting in the apartment of a guy who has a boyfriend from whom he's hiding my presence?

A few days later, I come back to Montreal with two of his Nike tank tops that I stole. Now, when I think back on it, I regret not having taken some young in-vogue designer's piece.

When Bert took my photo in the stall at Buttons after the soup, he was telling me that he was responsible for the casting at *Vogue* and that, *who knows?* if the photos came out well, there would maybe be a future for me in the business. I learned the hard way: no, the photos didn't turn out well, oh, and Bert, he's an asshole.

HOMEMADE PORNO
Berlin, Germany

It's the first second of a solo porn video that I filmed in the Berlin apartment I rented with Emma (sorry, babe, this is how I'm telling you). In the following moments, I perform a precise choreography, a choreography that I repeat at least eight times before collapsing from fatigue: I move back, I take off my shirt, I do three or four things that I don't want to describe here, and I aim for two minutes maximum to execute my routine.

All this because the day before, at Cocktail d'Amore, Sophy met a guy in the line she'd spent eight hours in before gaining entrance, whereas I — if I remember correctly — cut ahead of everyone with a group of French people. (The French were told no at the door, but not me, who entered in front of them as proud as anything.) The guy Sophy met is named Jacob, and, for a moment, I don't know why, I thought that he was the ugliest of the party. So I didn't pay attention to him.

That was Mistake #1. He was very handsome.

Cocktail — which no longer exists — was a huge, badly lit party where eighty thousand trained and sculpted biceps plowed into each other. Seriously, there wasn't a single person who wasn't shirtless and, after the first twenty-four hours, not a single person who wasn't in a jockstrap or a dog mask or something like that. Just saying, Sophy had discovered a secret mezzanine on the second floor and had become the dominatrix of the place. That was Cocktail for you.

Mistake #2: Telling Mika, Anton's friend, both of them dealers I met at Tresor a few days before, that we would go together to consult manuscripts at the Staatsbibliothek.

Basically, Mika turned out to be an expert on the Middle Ages; he tripped out on gold-painted initials, and he knew that Berlin houses a particularly famous manuscript that I'd seen the day before, for my studies. So Mika, whom I like a lot, kept me with him the whole evening in the hopes that I would accompany him to the library in the near future, which I already knew I wasn't going to do.

Anyway, it wasn't that big of a mistake, because I was entitled to two wingmen by my side, two masc-for-masc King Kong types who spend their days at the gym and who introduced me to their gang. Never again will I say something bad about douchebags, because to my great shock, everyone was real nice: they talked about the same things as us and I recall with delight everyone whom Anton introduced to me, Herculeses in leather Speedos who could have carried me, the beanpole, on their shoulders all evening without effort.

While we were wading through Cocktail, I ran face to face into Jacob, who seemed to be in a k-hole; right away, he took me by the hand and brought me under Sophy's mezzanine, in the immense slightly trashy dark room that scared me. We sat next to the line of guys waiting to go fuck a designated victim (a chosen one?), between a couple of folks in their forties who were finding each other at last after years of confusion, and some people searching for something on the ground, probably a dropped baggie of powder.

Incapable of speaking but extremely motivated to show me something, Jacob stuck out his tongue and his phone and began searching hastily through his photos, among more or less a thousand dick pics of himself and other guys, videos, and rather question-able selfies. Holding a photo of a normal penis, a little bigger than average, he pointed at himself, his tongue still out.

There ensued a weird sequence of events: Jacob, who wanted me to suck his dick, pointed from his mouth to his belt with his cell phone and placed the screen at an angle to indicate that it's *his* penis, all the while shaking a little. Miming understanding, I took his phone from his hands and gave him a kiss on the .jpeg. He jumped, saying *no no no* and started to unzip his pants to show me his flaccid penis.

At that moment, he regained the faculty of speech. He told me (in English, and I'm paraphrasing) *I would love if you kissed it, I'm too high on ketamine but my penis looks like what I showed you in the photo.* I let myself drop to the dirty floor of the dark room. I know that it would have been more dignified to say no, but nonetheless I chose to give him a cute little peck on the head of his penis — nothing that would wake the beast.

Mistake #3, the most fatal: Listening to him talk and letting myself be lulled by his wildest fantasies.

Jacob then measured two ml of GHB while explaining to me that he has a particular fetish: collecting face-dick pics. This type of photo is a powerful weapon that can put an end to anyone's political aspirations, because it's the only infallible way of associating the equipment with its owner and using their little intimacy against them. When he finished measuring the two ml of g, he warned me: *I'm going to go back to the state I was in fifteen minutes ago, so maybe we'd be better off separating.*

But don't forget me.

Which I didn't. I stayed a good twelve hours longer at Cocktail, and before leaving I headed back to Jacob with the goal of taking him with me. Except there were still another twelve hours before the party stopped, and he wanted to *socialize as much as possible*. Running with a particular idea, I went back to Neukölln, positioned myself in the room in front of the gorgeous luminous rays of the rising sun and I imagined my first solo porno.

Four hours later — I had technical issues filming the finale — I sent him the video. He must've still been at the party at that moment, but he replied immediately to tell me that the file was corrupted, that it wasn't working. I spent a half-hour reformatting the video so it would be compatible with his iPhone. I sent him the new file. Seen at 9:36 a.m. To this day, I still haven't had a response. If I'd known that, I would have put little golden initials all over my body — that might have worked better.

CUCUMBER
Mile End, Montreal

For a long time I looked for this exact photo because it's quite a funny souvenir: we're all at Glitterbomb, even Emma and Rouz, who don't usually like that kind of event. I'm completely blacked out, and as soon as everyone is ready to go back to the house, I climb into a taxi occupied by four random girls who scream at me to get out.

Except I refuse to get out, and I demand that everyone calm themselves because IT'S NOT WORTH GETTING WORKED UP LIKE THAT, I'M JUST BLACKED OUT AND DON'T KNOW WHERE I AM ANYMORE. Luckily for me, there's a girl in the back who tells the others to stop screaming, *look how pathetic he is*. But pathetic or not, what happens is that in the front, real cozy next to the taxi driver, I'm taking up the place of the fourth friend who from the outside is hitting me with her high heel through the open window.

I'm kicked out on the curb next to Emma and Rouz, whose jaws are on the floor seeing me expelled like this. By mutual agreement, we decide to go to Cyberia—Jacob accepts without really realizing it, I think. The after-party is much more crowded than usual, but, seized by a stroke of genius, I figure I'm going to show my stamp from Glitterbomb to skip the line and avoid paying the cover. I was the only one who managed it: Emma, Rouz, and Jacob (actually quite pissed off) go back to the house and leave me alone at Cyberia.

Which means I'm ALONE, BLACKED OUT, probably OUT OF MONEY, and everything that happens there is unpublished; no one knows the series of events that is deeply embedded in an inaccessible part of my brain.

I imagine that there was Valentin, Oli, the usual gang who dropped in—I can't really say. I only know that I regain consciousness right in the middle of the street, at seven in the morning, like an old cucumber, accompanied by Aubrey, Sean, and Bobby, who reassure the Instagram community by announcing that they've finally found me.

A little messed up, we sit/spread out on the sidewalk at the corner of Parc and Van Horne while the sun rises. It's one of the last hot days of the fading summer, and I have my head on Sean whose head is on Aubrey whose head is on Bobby who is saying that after-parties, they don't really have any use, other than spending moments between friends lying against one another.

WEDNESDAY
Neukölln, Berlin

Middle of the week I'm among the plants it's sunny
in our little one zimmer in Neukölln I'm crying telling Emma that I'm going back to sleep all afternoon
to replenish my serotonin which has evaporated.

THE QUEEN OF THE TOILETS
Berghain / Panorama Bar

On LoremIpsum's Instagram, with a little searching, one can readily find the marine Aquarius Zelda swamp fairy symbolism that Sophy and I recognized at Berghain the first time we spent an evening there together. In this club, which is like an amusement park for adults, there are three floors where different groups cohabit. In the second artery of the third floor, to the left, the cool kids of Generation Instagram assemble. Not much there, just two toilets and a bench, but it's big enough for a handful of youth — whom Sophy and I know virtually — to gather.

(If everyone meets up at the toilets, it's because that's the ideal place to do keta. Nothing mysterious or coincidental: it's drugs that organize the space at Berghain.)

We found the spot — which we will thereafter call "the oasis" because it will serve to revitalize us — by shuffling like zombies after beautiful people with familiar haircuts: bowl cut like me, bangs and mullet cut like Sophy, bleached hair, middle part vagina cut, chrome dome, etc. We were following the tufts like a token of possible friendship by placing ourselves strategically behind them in the line for the toilets, striking up a conversation at the opportune moment. Seeing as we had hair compatible with theirs, the tufts started to talk to us. Bingo.

That's how we met LoremIpsum, a beauty of a siren who's dangerous because she's hypnotizing. Hair slicked with oil running on her transparent beige top, it looked like she'd just left the pool and had come directly to dance. There was also Chad, a little skater wearing Gosha Rubchinskiy whom I'd also noticed on the dance floor. Because of the keta of the m of the ecstasy of the speed no one spoke, but we all interpreted the silence as proof of composure and self-control. My Gosha shirt winked at Chad's, recognizing its counterpart.

Inside, we exchanged lines (my keta for their m), and I took love potion for the first time, not even a micro-dose. Don't think that I find it glamorous, the love potion: it's really dangerous because every time I took some I fell in love *for real*, and that cost me thousands of dollars in trips from one city to another in the world. (How many trees I'd have to plant to offset my ecological footprint because of that, I don't know anymore.)

So everything was great, but Sophy and I wanted to take maximum advantage of the fifteen-minute window during which all the drugs would come together in harmony. We went to Panorama to see I don't remember what anymore, and when the mixture lost its effect, we returned to the oasis to realize that the whole little group was still there: the cool kids hadn't moved an inch and they were still smiling mindlessly while waiting for a stall. LoremIpsum too, still splendid, tall and ethereal, hair still as damp as before, but let's just say Sophy and I started to find it bizarre when we rejoined the line and our silence resumed its usual course, right where we'd left it. So they never went to dance?

Under the faint techno 4/4 in the distance, everyone struggled to shape the lines of keta as precisely as possible and to make the most perfect parallels (the kind that would never touch if they continued on infinitely). I was given another two ml of love potion, and Sophy and I took off to wander the first floor where I ran into Florian, with whom I did not need a potion to *actually* fall in love, but that'll be a tale for another time.

Long story short, when we came back round somewhere in the chilling area called Säule, we gathered up our things, realigned our legs to our bodies (damn keta), then returned to the third-floor toilets where, surprise, surprise, the whole insta crew were still waiting. It was troubling to see that nothing had changed. Whether we were there or not, it all played out in the same way. The Gosha and Lorem's two beige-covered breasts smiled complicitly at us, and, without question, we got back on the merry-go-round, as seasoned as we were.

The measures the silence the parallels the precision strung together, Sophy looked at me as though to say *what are we doing here* and, by mutual agreement, we went down to the Berghain dance floor, where Ben Klock was ringing the midnight bells in his DJ set. We told each other we would never go back up to the toilets again.

Since that day, I have the impression that the Instagram generation is gifted with a particularly strong intuition, a sixth sense that alerts a user when they're starting to drop in popularity, because as though they had sensed that we were beginning to judge them, the members of the second artery gang came down to Berghain's main dance floor just as the lighting took on a blue tinge that seemed to anticipate their arrival.

Like a Marie Antoinette of the underground, Lorem was sitting on her throne in the centre of the club just next to us. We understood that she who didn't seem to have a life outside Instagram was studying dance. She and her group of friends were getting ready to do their show.

I'm not kidding: they placed a bottle of water in the centre of the dance floor and their bodies gravitated around the gold of the future, following a beat that was completely out of sync with the music. We all gravitated a little with them. (Shame on me: while doing their little show, they leaned toward the bottle as though to pick it up, and, wanting to do the right thing, I held it out to them because I thought the drugs were preventing them from grabbing it. Their gorgeous smiles led me to understand that it was a prop in their performance and that I should put the bottle back down in the middle of the crowd so that the dance could continue.)

And in the blue lights that flooded Berghain, the club kids' honour was safe. It was such a strange dance that I have trouble describing it; it was like the performance given by a fairy mid-transformation. Because of the humidity that they'd created around themselves, Lorem's hair had spread out in very big curls, and Sophy told me the next day that, when the whole thing had concluded, she'd dreamed that we had emerged with great difficulty from a deep swamp where we'd stayed too long. It wasn't entirely false.

IN THE METRO
Montreal, Quebec

Is he gay because he's looking at me or is he looking
at me because I'm gay?

HOW I LEARNED TO DANCE
Club Unity, Montreal

It was the time of Sour Puss shooters, blackouts, and a questionable fashion style: apple-green shirts and other whimsies of that sort.

You sure you wanna do this? Emma had asked in front of the Tim Hortons in the Village while we drank vodka poured into a bottle of orange juice much too small for the quantity of alcohol that we'd put there. *I feel like I'm going to lose my baby*, she added.

Yes, I was ready for my first entrance into Unity. I'd been ready for months, ever since I'd heard that the music major gang went there while little fifteen-year-old me — who'd just come out — hadn't yet set foot inside. That evening, the stars were aligned for me to enter the major leagues.

It's JF—who probably doesn't remember—who'd helped me create my fake ID for Dono's birthday. He knew a friend of a friend of a friend who knew a guy who did a little trafficking in hyperrealistic (paper) cards that just had to be slid into the see-through slot of a wallet to be shown with pride at the entrance of the U. (It's certain that the bouncer saw through our little game, but apparently there was a market for twinks inside.)

Emma was bawling like the mother of Christ seeing her son on the cross, but I'd already moved on to other things in my life, ready to french left and right, to drink to death, to have the best and worst encounters of my life; I couldn't stand to wait any longer. I placed two kisses on her tears, I looked her in the eyes, and I lied to her: *We'll see each other at school everything will be the same you'll see I won't have changed one bit.*

Except that walking toward the U, I had the impression of having grown to my adult height in three seconds. It must have been the card having this effect on me: the brazen thing even said that I was twenty-three years old (we hadn't taken any chances on the age, and I'd learned my new zodiac sign by heart—Scorpio). I think I was wearing a too-tight sickeningly green T-shirt—a colour that never came back in fashion. The bouncer distractedly compared my face with the photo on the card (a real photo of me, that was the advantage of JF's contact) and he told me *Awaye, get in here.*

You always remember the tune that was playing when you entered the U for the first time. "Stronger" by Kanye West; I listen to it again to write my field notes. It was spectacular; something really must have been at work for that to have been the tune that played as I entered. I was reinvigorated by this hit, which was already old at the time and which gave me the necessary energy to face this vast unknown world that I would soon know like the back of my hand.

In the crowd, I couldn't make anyone out and the music major gang wasn't exactly mine, so I had to find allies ASAP. Luckily, on the first floor, between big blocks where people climb up to dance — a trial of style and technique that I wasn't going to attempt right away — between the lesbians' corner and the little bar for shooters, there were girls whom I knew by name, who'd been going out as a group from the age of twelve and supposedly had a lot of "experience."

There was a girl among them who was familiar to me: Manue, an angel fallen from heaven who quickly swept me along through the three floors and explained to me how the space is divided by showing me places where I might be a hit and those where I was short a beard and a paunch to enter, mentioning in passing that for *us*, it was the second floor, kingdom of the PCD and Britney. In less than three minutes, we'd drunk five shots of vodka and I was dancing as best as I could in a room that wasn't dark enough for my taste.

Let's talk right away about the numerous mistakes that I made during that first club evening: thinking that the clip of the song "1, 2 Step" by Ciara, which I'd discovered by typing *club music* on YouTube, constituted a dance lesson sufficient for a beanpole low-key nerd who struggled to walk straight without colliding with a coat rack or dropping something, who had put on big poorly fitting Sorel boots and forgot my belt while wearing pants two sizes too big. All this must've made me seem really at ease on the dance floor...

The absence of the belt, we're going to admit it, really played out in my favour. During "Buttons" by the Pussycat Dolls, as I was going *huh huh* with my face, I lowered my head right to the floor and lifted it back up languorously while making sure to display the goods, and a quite mature man — I'd say not old-old, but at least twice my fifteen years almost sixteen — approached from behind. I instantly gave Manue an accusatory look like, WTF *how do I react here?* She told me, as an excellent initiator to sexuality: *Let it happen, it's fun!*

I think that a part of me pressed up against the guy to become closer to Manue and to have something to talk about Monday at school. At the exact moment I felt him grind into my back, I was already hard, and it didn't take much time for him to put his hands in my pants. I don't think we frenched, rather it was completely mechanical — which didn't bother me, it must be said. I barely spoke, too happy to return to Manue and recount what had happened. It really made a big impression on me when she didn't react to my story, she who had already heard all those of Dono, of her boyfriend at the conservatory, and of JF, who hadn't come out at the time but who was already the queen of the U.

The evening ended too quickly, and I came home through the window (which really wasn't necessary because my dad didn't worry too much about those sorts of things). The next day, I was stalking Dono and JF on Facebook, only to find out that months earlier they had posted a photo of an after-party at the home of the guy who'd touched me, a random dude who must've been pushing forty, whom I'd been reassured afterwards was fine but had the shortcoming of chilling with boys far too young who'd been falsely certified as adults with their pretty paper IDs. I wasn't yet aware of the ethical questions raised by the event; I was just pleased to enter the network of sluts and to have been touched by someone who'd also touched some of my friends.

GLITTERBOMB
Montreal, Quebec

Fall asleep naked glitter on the face and all over the covers around six or seven in the morning.

Be woken barely a few hours later by the cries of a little girl eight years of age max: *Mommy, there's a naked man in the bed!*

Fuck. We were renting our apartment out on Airbnb and my roomie forgot to tell me.

Allô, petite fille.

PLEASE DON'T JUMP OFF THE BRIDGE
Montreal, Quebec

Twenty-four hours before the fateful moment, I am home copying the makeup of an old Palomo Spain catalogue. It consists of a ton of turquoise around the eyes, a bit of shimmer in the corner, a darker blue under the eye, and pink or a delicate colour as highlight. I put it all together with a glitter crop top bought the day before and little blue Adidas shorts. Simple, effective: I love it.

We must be a thousand people meeting for Glitterbomb, arrayed with a clever mix of rare pearls bought in thrift stores and materials we spotted prepared concocted with the goal of, I dunno, cruising and bringing someone back home, probably. Jacob and me, we'd already drunk twenty beers and the wolf pack wanted to do MDMA. I no longer really have memories of the party, but there are lots and lots of photos on my phone of all the make-out groups that formed while we were slumped on the sidewalk and the curb of Rue Jean-Talon (to the great displeasure of the vehicles that were honking at us): Jake with me, Jake with Max, Max with Zach and Marie, Zach with Jake, Jake with Marc, Marc with Marie and Jake and Max and me, Jake with everyone, and so on, but it's all there in our phones, caked makeup and bleary eyes.

At the bar's closing time, we realize that we took in zero of the evening, that we want more of it, and Alej (who'd frenched no one?) tells us that he has beer at his place and that we should go to Durocher; it's said to be the event of the century every week and, if I recall correctly, there was a really special DJ that we all wanted to see so yes we went toward Parc-Ex, eyes closed legs shaky.

The talk of the evening was Marc, who'd just returned from London with an incredible quantity of clothing that he'd found/stolen left and right and that he'd resewn to his taste with his young up-and-coming designer eye. It gave him a complex out-of-sync look, and the guy was hot. En route to Durocher, we sat in an alley and staged a fashion show. *Walk, walk, fashion baby, work it, move that bitch crazy,* three hundred more photos of Alej's sunglasses and a mesh top north of the train track.

Right: the track. Still intoxicated and exhausted from having done at least two hours of cat-walking, we decide to take the shortcut and hop the fence. By mutual agreement even though I hesitate — *that might be dangerous* — we move forward through the foliage, Jake and Marc lose their phones by putting their fanny packs down on the path, we progress, we progress, Alej jumps, Marc jumps, Ayisha jumps, I jump, but of course my wrist gets caught in the little spikes at the top of the twelve-foot fence as I swan-dive off.

Adrenaline and all, I try to relativize the state of my wrist, which is entirely open right next to some tendons and veins. Everyone flips out except me. Big debate on the possibility that I go or don't go to the after-party I campaign for yes, the whole universe is against my idea, we put it to a vote, on *no* all hands in the air except my open wrist, I agree to go to Rosemont hospital, terribly disappointed to be separated from the gang. Jake comes with me even though Ayisha (too cute) offered, although we had just met.

Five in the morning, I make my entrance to the hospital like a diva in the glitter crop top, a little wide-eyed thanks to the end of the m, makeup still caked — but fabulous — clashing very visibly with the severe flus and various accidents. I cradle my wrist and rapidly estimate the number of people that are there, to evaluate the possibility of my return to the after-party before it ends.

There follows a funny progression through the hospital world where my state is tolerated to various degrees. The security guard at the entrance tells me to approach and give my information, but he doesn't dare look at me for a second and, when I give him my ID with my good wrist, he insists that I place it in front of me.

I admire the guts of the triage nurse who, on the verge of asking me the usual questions, says, indicating my look: *Non. Non. This, this doesn't fly. You've gone too far, là.* We remained in a respectful silence, two polite clans accepting to rule in discord. I had to enumerate the drugs consumed over the course of the evening like I was in the confessional of a Christian church in the thirteenth century.

After having waited in the room for around an hour — an hour drawing the edges of my skin together — I went in to see the doctor, who asked me to sit and with whom I chatted for a long time openly about the after-party scene in Montreal and her shitty shift during which she was alone managing the drunks and the drugged all night. I took a selfie like a rock star, wrist bloody, apparently dying. The doctor froze my wrist, four stitches and it was done. Out.

We took a taxi and went directly to the after-party while the sun gave colour back to the city.

Don't talk about this night with my mother. I could die.

CUCUMBER (THE REAL STORY)
Mile End, Montreal

The first time that I wanted to write this story, I choked before the end. I'm trying again.

Around seven in the morning, still high on ketamine, I return from Cyberia and can't get to sleep. I open Grindr, and the only person online is Bobby, whom I'd just left at the after-party. We message each other to say *there are NOT plenty of fish in the sea, apparently*. If a top had been looking for a bottom, there would've been a fight over him.

I throw my phone on the bed and start typing some nonsense in a Word document without it really working. Because of the drugs I have a sort of blockage; usually, I write and it all comes out of my head like trickling logorrhea.

Five minutes later, frustrated, I go into the kitchen and get a Lebanese cucumber out of the fridge. I tell myself that if no one wants to fuck me, I'm going to take care of it myself. Like an adult. Only the cucumber is too cold and even if I put it between the bed and my stomach a good fifteen seconds to warm it up, it still feels like an iceberg when I put it in my ass.

Suddenly, I think of a solution. I put the cucumber in the microwave a few seconds — no more, can't have it go soft. I take it out, as satisfied as Arthur pulling the sword from the stone, and I return to my room, victorious.

I always preferred penises to toys, but that morning, a cucumber did the job.

KETAMINE
Berghain / Panorama Bar

I regain consciousness tranquilly under the hot sun of a Sunday afternoon. I realize that I'm bare-chested, that I still have my shorts (lucky), and that I'm lying on a metal islet, head oriented toward the grey clouds threatening to burst in the distance. Oscar (whom I'd forgotten) enters my bubble and points to a guy dancing under the water features of Berghain's interior garden. The guy's handsome, it's true. He struts his stuff in the middle of a crowd that gathered at four in the afternoon for the set of Honey Dijon — a DJ everyone admires — while consuming drug cocktails.

It's funny to watch the little ants circulating below, with their bleached hair, dark see-through shirts, and eyes that no longer really focus thanks to the ketamine, while it would have been the perfect day — thirty-two degrees Celsius — to go to the beach or to Weißer See, the little lake at the centre of Berlin. Only none of these people will ever miss Sunday at Berghain — it's a quasi-spiritual rendezvous for the local techno addicts.

(Nevertheless, that was one of my favourite activities, sitting outside on Sundays listening to the DJs who usually play bubblier music than the hard techno that blasts inside. I spent hours gazing at familiar faces below while imagining to myself the details of their lives, already thinking a little of the field notes that I wanted to write.)

Oscar looks at his watch and tells me we're due for another bump, to which I agree without much thought. We climb down from the promontory to go countercurrent through the crowd that faces the DJ booth, while I become aware and a little embarrassed of the fact that I'm not wearing a shirt. Oscar sees my arms raised to try and hide my tits: *Relax, you look worse if you don't fully own it.* He's not wrong. Except that Oscar has a metabolism like fire and he works out a few days a week; heads turn when he arrives at Berghain with his gang of boys who had eggs dusted with speed for breakfast, preparing themselves mentally and physically for the Sunday Classic...

Walking toward the toilets, I look around for Ben without success, Ben to whom I'd just bid an early farewell before his departure to Sweden, where he's returning to study. But in the Berghain crowd, I don't manage to find him. He's isolating himself somewhere, I know it, and pretends to have forgotten how his phone functions. Oscar tells me that at this time, one must think of one's personal pleasure and leave others to live their lives. Okay.

The more my Sunday progresses, the more often I feel I see him appear before me in the crowd or the bend of a hallway or sitting on a little bench at the café where they sell ice cream on the third floor. My mind is split in two the whole rest of the day due to the disappointment of having come to see him and having missed him. Once you lose someone in the caverns of Berghain, yeah, good luck finding them again.

Oh well. I sink deeper into the line for one of the first-floor toilets. I say hi to some regulars who must also consider me a regular by now, we don't say more than two proper sentences but we're happy to see each other, then Oscar brings me inside a stall and closes the door, takes out his materials, card, straw, phone, forms more or less reasonable lines—*I'm working early tomorrow so this might be my last round*, he says to me. He sniffs his, I gather up the rest, ready set go in forty-five minutes the buzz will be gone.

Instantly, I sense my interior geography take a hit, my mental map of Berghain shifts like the staircases at Hogwarts that buzz off just to annoy the students.

I lose sight of Oscar while I ponder things that have the vastness of a galaxy, that swirl like atoms in my head. I don't exactly know what I'm doing here.

(I decided to come to Berlin the day after meeting Ben: while we walked close to the ballet studio in Montreal, he explained to me that he was leaving in a week but that he'd be happy to see me if I were thinking of touring around Germany, which I said I would somewhat on a whim after talking to Emma about it and buying frankly not very expensive tickets, thanks to Wow Air.)

Later, still feeling raw but less and less so, I rouse myself to realize that I'm now with Anton and Mika, the muscly gorillas and superfine dealers that I've already talked about. They stick to each other on the stage in the gay section of the dance floor, next to the dark rooms. Mika points to a dude and tells me that that's his husband: a shocking revelation because Mika isn't gay. He explains that to flee Russia, he had to get married, which was easier to do with his American best friend than to concoct another plan. And that all told, that's the person he appreciates the most in life, so why not *put a ring on it?*

To be honest, I start to be a little disconcerted by the radical change that happens in the evening that I would have wanted to dedicate to Ben: the clock hits eleven and the club is jam-packed. I assume that Oscar left and that he abandoned the idea of finding me again to give me a kiss. I follow Anton and Mika toward the toilets, where we wait an hour in line. A&M greet half the people who go this way because they know everyone, they're nice and they introduce me left and right. Slowly but surely, we progress toward the end of a tunnel: the metal interior of the non-functional toilets decorated by a designer to seem trashy.

Time stops.

I was in the same place, in the same stall, a month and a half earlier. I was wearing an ugly baseball cap borrowed from Ben and I was with Lili, whom I didn't know but who was taking care of me by offering me some lines (*put some k in a big euro note fold crush unfold slip onto the phone*). This evening, doing more keta but with Anton and Mika, I remember that moment precisely, the sound of the plastic of a card that squeaks on a phone and that I could have tasted. This synesthetic sensation is imprinted in my head by direct association.

Mika turns back to me: *Want some more?*

My heart is spinning like a comet that's going to crash into the earth.

Leaving the stall, I think I see Ben in the distance turning on the dance floor.

MIDNIGHT IN PARIS
Paris, France

Bert and I are in the same city on February 28, almost six months to the day after we first met.

I return from Morocco and spend twenty-four hours double-quick in Paris. I vaguely plan to see a museum in the evening, come back to the apartment that I rented on Airbnb, and call it a day. Of course, that's not what happens.

Mathieu, gorgeous little imp, invites me to He.She. They, a queer party that takes place during Fashion Week. At first, I suggest to him that we dress undressed and go be all the rage at the Palais de Tokyo, but the more we think about it, the less we're tempted by the idea of being shirtless in tight little blue shorts in the middle of an exhibition. We skip the contemporary art to go drink vodka in a McDo, where I try everything on the Parisian menu not available in Montreal. (In case you're interested, the Croque McDo is insane.)

For fun, I text Bert, *Come and meet us, we'll wait for you*. No response. He's clearly with the models, backstage.

In general, I have a poor tolerance for vodka. I forget that it's really strong, and I go full headless chicken. We must have visited twenty terraces of little bars, Mathieu and I, before joining Clément in a grocery where they sell cheap pastis and bad beer, but poppers of superior quality — hence the appeal of the place. We choose to treat ourselves to a bottle of each colour: for Clément, the red one, because it's less strong and he's working the next day; for Mathieu, the blue, the one that unclenches the anus the best; for me, the black, the strongest.

Before losing my bearings, I text Bert to keep him up to date on our intersection, *Faubourg and Château d'eau, in the tenth, near Chez Jeannette*. I presume that he knows that bar, an "institution" according to my friends, because it's there that Gaspar Noé chills, and he only chills with models, apparently.

The poppers were really strong. I find myself shouting my loves to Notre-Dame, with Clément and Mathieu who are fifty times less inebriated than me. In girl-squad mode, we invade the party, whose guest list we'd obtained thanks to Mathieu, who got cruised by the organizer the day before. Except that the moment we enter the club, we decide to hide bottles of spirits in our underwear, which the bouncer immediately noticed. Now that I think back on it, our ploy must have been evident, but at the time, I felt that we'd just barely missed the mark.

Once inside, but without the bottles, I text Bert again: *Come, it's amazing in here!*

It's not as amazing as all that: there must be about fifty people here. We really get the impression of having passed right by the trendy spot where the cool kids should be. Nonetheless, because of Fashion Week, the gang is magnificent, but all its members, barely legal. In less than thirty minutes, we become the stars of the place, the youngsters lining up to come see us. The fact is that we reek of poppers and that the fashion world is completely addicted to them.

Each time that I take a sniff, I black out for a good thirty seconds. After, I come back into the world, but elsewhere in the bar. Rinse and repeat. From the dance floor, I come to in the toilets with new friends. We sniff together, a good minute passes, I find myself at the bar with fifteen shooters in front of me for these people who became my best friends. I flip out a little; I reluctantly agree to pay the bill.

I get out the Prada wallet that Jake gave me for my birthday — a wallet that's consistently worth more than what's found inside — and I hand my credit card to the bartender. Declined. She doesn't look happy. I swear to her that I'm not short on funds — I just gave a course and the finances are, after seven years of poverty, actually going rather well. She tries again. She's very happy to tell me that it still doesn't work.

It's expired.

I take the card and observe that it was set to expire after February 28, 2019. My phone tells me that it's one minute past midnight, the first of March — the transaction was one minute from going through. A guy behind me says he's going to pick up the bill. *Don't worry, I'm rich as fuck.* I have faith in him, happily. Anyhow, I just avoided paying eighty-four euros for fifteen shooters.

The shots don't help my pitiful state. I tell the guys that we should look for Bert and his friends, that they must be at another party. Clément replies that it's impossible, but after a bit of research on his iPhone, he finds a bit of a lesser-known place, more edgy. *Chances are good that they'd be there.*

Bert, I'm coming! God.

He isn't there; nonetheless we still had lots of fun wandering in the labyrinths of a party visibly influenced by what's going on in Berlin.

Bert, where are youuu?

I no longer have money, and I have to walk all the way to my apartment, at the other end of the earth, near the Père-Lachaise cemetery.

I'm still up to party if you want to.

The sun is rising. My flight is in two hours.

U up?

Damn poppers.

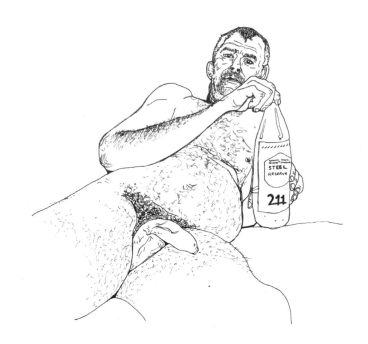

CHATROULETTE
Bar le Stud, Montreal

Seen with my own two eyes: sitting completely naked in front of a slot machine, a seventy-something daddy masturbating while facing a group of uncomfortable twinks. When he grasps that the audience isn't right, he adds a twenty to the machine and plays Cats Royal.

TWO FOR ONE
Montreal, Quebec

I'm seeing double. I don't know if it's because of the big pitchers ordered at l'Escalier or if it's just because I'm really happy to be with Samuelle and Thomas, but I'm seeing double and having a hard time walking straight. There are people dancing too intensely to trash rock and there are probably some UQAM initiations going down in this pseudo-edgy bar in which I will never again set foot after this evening.

To pop my eyes back into their respective sockets, Thomas offers me two lines as long as my hand, one for each nostril, which he draws on the table in the big room in the back to the left. I no longer know if we got side-eyed because we cut it out in the open. Once the lines are consumed, I glimpse stars. At least I'm starting to see clearly again.

Eyes watering, I raise my head toward Thomas to thank him and, at the next table over, I notice a really cute guy who's looking at me. Not because of the drugs, no: he's looking at me because he finds me cute. I leap from my chair as quick as possible, energized by the coke that is already taking effect.

I propel myself toward him, head tilted to give him pecks on the cheek. He doesn't seem bothered by my angle of approach, so we talk about everything and nothing, about what we do for a living, *studies, studies for me too*, we find each other attractive, we add each other on Instagram, then we devour each other with our eyes.

Having finished the rounds of the easy subjects, we agree on a plan: we go home in order to devour each other with more than our eyes. With the snap of a finger, Sam and Thomas agree on a similar plan. Outside, we piss next to the magazine store Multimags, and my new lover reveals to us that he'd only just turned eighteen the day before: huge discomfort.

We all go home together nonetheless by taking the bus on Saint-Denis. It's there that I realize that we're being followed by another guy, who's been tracking us since the bar. I recognize him because we already exchanged dick pics on Hornet, intelligence that I immediately yell at Sam. An excellent wingwoman, she goes toward him and asks him to describe himself in three brief sentences. He's called Valentin, he hates Valentine's Day, but he likes cinnamon hearts.

Thomas, Sam, Valentin, the young one, and I introduce ourselves in turn, then I find it pertinent to
repeat really really loudly that he and I already know
each other by interchanged penile images. People
exclaim uncomfortably on the bus, and some of them
change places.

During this time, I manage to make advances on
both guys alternately, in case my barely legal boy
decides to leave us. My flirting works too well and we
crowd into the apartment Sam and I rent on Saint-
André to drink the gin of our other roomie (we're
still apologizing) and to offer lines left and right.

Fed up with waiting, the young one takes me by the
hand and brings me toward my room, where we suck
each other off a bit, but I'm too put out about miss-
ing the party so I ask him, patting him on the head,
to be patient for a minute. I re-emerge victorious,
half-naked, and swallow gin in big glassfuls.

And so, Valentin, I feel bad informing you of this,
but when you brought me toward the kitchen under
the pretext that you were hungry and we sucked each
other off on the counter, it was my second blowjob
of the evening. I think that we weren't quick enough
because the young almost-minor became aware of
our scheme and came to glare at us. We laughed a
bit, and I didn't see him again when I returned to
the living room.

The party stretched on into the wee hours of the morning. At the end, we took photos in which I look like a little goober who knows what he's just done. I'm shirtless and everyone's more excited than normal. The next day, I realized that the young one blocked me on Instagram, and I haven't tried to contact him since.

DIRTY SHOES
Berlin, Germany

The results of the laboratory analysis identified on my shoes that famous mix of "brown" substances that are found everywhere on the dark-room floors of Paris and Berlin: mud, sweat, cigarette butts, sperm, and worse still. My shoes carry the stain of a tour of Europe in eighty days accomplished not in a hot air balloon, but rather with Wow Air (which just went bankrupt).

What the results of the analysis didn't detect: in Paris, while searching with difficulty for an ecstasy pill, Mathieu and I stop in front of the sketchy vendor who always stays close to the toilets, and, with a nod, he tells us: *If you're walking here, at this hour and in this place, it's because you desire something you don't have, and that thing, I can provide it to you.*

Dumbstruck by his completely unexpected eloquence for a dealer, we follow him to a stall in which the toilet has overflowed; HORS SERVICE is written on the door.

Feet in the dirty water, proud to tell us, *Lucky day: I've got two ecsta pills left*, the dealer drops the first in the toilet juice on the floor. It's Mathieu who swallows that one. It had begun to dissolve on contact with the shit and other excretions.

After, we make ourselves a line in the palm of the dealer's hand with the crumbs lingering in the bottom of his baggie of e.

Another thing missed by the laboratory that analyzed my shoes: the (numerous) expeditions that Jacob and I carried out into the dark rooms of Pornceptual.

The first: To discover. Habituate our eyes to the darkness.

The second, one or two hours later: *To just see the type of person who's in there*, as Jacob announced. We suck each other off anyway in the back of the room, where not much is happening.

The third, fifteen minutes later: To fuck, channelling the energy of the party that's starting to take effect. We soon become a sort of attraction when Jacob gives me a rim job, tongue dug deep between my parted ass cheeks. Dozens of bodies cluster around us, and I must admit that there are certain moments of confusion. Thinking that Jacob is really going to town eating my ass, I carefully jerk him off behind me, his hard cock in my hands, realizing after several minutes that he's actually IN FRONT OF ME. Scared, I exit the dark room running and bump right into my friend Dillon and his boyfriend. Mini discomfort as I try to make small talk all while hiding my erection in my blue Nike shorts. I nonetheless get myself out alright.

(A little later, a guy comes to ask me if I recognize him: *No*. He puts my hand on his peen — I left without saying anything. I recognized him in a second.)

Last thing that the laboratory analysis didn't detect: at Berghain, our friend Jean-Christian, who is veeeeeeeeeeery happy to see us, asks us if we have some k. *Yes*, bada bing, bada boom, we find ourselves in the dark room, the most convenient place to make ourselves a key bump. Jean-Christian slips away immediately after; I find myself once more alone with Jacob. Because we are a bit disoriented and we can't see further than the tips of our noses — it's not called a *dark* room for nothing — we really struggle to pass each other the key. I drop some powder and let out a big loud *oops*; Jacob interprets my cry of distress as the signal that I dropped the key and he leans to pick up the first thing that he could find on the ground: a *disgusting*, old, wet paper — I don't even want to think about what soaked it. I hear a strange sound, like breaking glass, and I imagine right away that Jacob gathered a shattered pane with his bare hands.

Needless to say, we left real quick.

So that's that. I also went to the Sahara with those shoes, maybe that purified them. Jacob wasn't too happy when I came back from the desert, because they were shoes that he'd lent me, telling me, *Be really careful with them, please.*

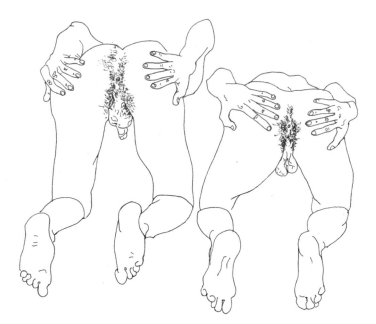

SAD BOYS
Montreal, Quebec

There's no object that doesn't think only of shining.

It's this quote from Pierre Lapointe, though distorted, that is pronounced to me by a quite well-known photographer as he pushes me against a white wall to take my photo; no time to think about my pose. Six in the morning, I'm on the brink of fainting because of my second MD. We're at Eastern Bloc. The headhunter is looking to cast new guys for his modelling agency.

I seem like a walking corpse; I'm pale and bothered in the photo. That's maybe what he's looking for: the "heroin chic" style, little ravers who have three-day under-eye circles and a bony silhouette because they don't eat enough.

He looks at my photo, doesn't seem really satisfied, but gives me his card anyway, a white square on which I see his name, an @ followed by the name of the agency, and a phone number to text him later. He's smiling and flirts with me, and, for an instant, I think that it may be a project that will happen. Like all the young gays who flaunt themselves in selfies on Instagram, I hope that one day I'm discovered and considered a work of art.

Maybe it'll happen — the agency will select me and a brilliant career awaits me — maybe he's talking to me simply because he wants to fuck me. One or the other. Not both. Photographers are dangerous because they exert a crazy power over young people like me.

The next day, the weather is mega-beautiful. I'm hung over on my balcony under a too-strong sun, and I look proudly at his business card. I wrote to all my friends to relive the moment in writing. I decide to contact the photographer, who's probably not awake. I barely slept, and I got up early to not completely miss the light. *Hey! We met yesterday, I don't know if you remember me, but here's my number.*

To my great surprise, he replies right away: *Thanks for texting.* Nothing else. I waited all afternoon to see if he was going to say more. Several days later, exasperated, I send him some nonsense so he'll put me back in his mind, three or four words. No reply.

I waited a really long time for the shitty goddamn photo that he took pushing me against the white wall of Eastern Bloc to be published on Facebook so I could answer the questions that were killing me: Do I have a weird grin because of the stress? Are my eyes rolling back into my head because of the MD? The photographer finally shared it a month after the party: all my friends commented on it, and I was tagged a thousand times even though I kept untagging myself. I don't look half-bad — in the photo. But not exceptional, on the other hand.

The photographer never called me back. I'm not photogenic enough, not relaxed enough in front of the camera to be represented by an agency.

But attractive enough for him to want to eat my ass.

THE ISLAND OF LESBOS — GREECE
Villeray, Montreal

Parc Jarry on the peninsula, a mix of ket and mush makes me see the most beautiful of sunsets. Twenty people return from a very long rave at Durocher, their smiles prominent, having had a great time. Another twenty get up after a good night's sleep; the people are reinvigorated, but worried about having missed something.

I take Marine and Jacqui's picture, proud on a rock tagged "hoes"; theirs is a devastating beauty thanks to the rays of the golden hour. Marine, too beautiful in her big black pants, her tight sleeveless top and her nylon belt, jumps toward me to approve the photo on the screen of my phone.

In the distance, I see Sophy, dressed in yellow with little flowers on her collar, laughing but probably realizing that the sunset marks the end of her two weeks with Marine, who came to Montreal to love her, who will leave again just as quickly when autumn begins to set in.

We take even more ket and even more photos, have even more mush and even more love; I go see Anas, short hair, grating vibe, who tells me that we're short on everything. It's my mission to ensure that the evening continues; I accept because I like this type of challenge.

With the aim of borrowing her bike, I talk to Emma — white-haired siren — who tells me *yes*, but that *it would be easier with Camille's bike*, brilliant lipstick trimmed hair tucked behind her ears.

I pedal as fast as possible, fast because I don't want to miss anything, fast to the point of busting my face in at the intersection of Jean-Talon and Parc, which is truly designed like shit; the cars never let bikes go through, fucking what, I never should have accepted: my house is really far from Parc Jarry, after all.

On the way back, triumphant because beers keta and more mush, I lift the bike in my arms to jump from one rock to the other, I arrive in front of Ayisha with glasses out of *The Matrix* and the je-ne-sais-quoi of Sansa Stark, who welcomes me with praises worthy of Sappho.

Speaking of Sappho, I realize that there are only girls left on the peninsula. I go toward Leticia, whom I can no longer see very well in the dark and who gives me a bit of hummus. I kiss everyone and decide to leave them to themselves. The ride was too long, and I sobered up.

I will later learn that the seven beautiful sirens finished the evening in an orgy, between the cattails, on the picnic tables, right up until the guy who picks up empty bottles came to interrupt them. That didn't prevent them from concluding it somewhere else.

BAHNHOF ZOO
Montreal, Quebec

My first experimentations with drugs were fed by the strangest things.

Ben takes a caffeine pill — it's yellow — and crushes it into immense lines that make us bleed from the nose. Of course, I do them for love; I'm more trying to impress than to stay awake. The thing with caffeine is that it works super well, and this electrifies us for the entire weekend.

We're celebrating the departure of Ben, whom I only just met. That weekend, I discover everything: the location of all the after-parties in Montreal, the raves, · the different effects created by drug combinations, the intense lack of sleep. I learn to trust my friends when I black out and when I no longer know where my feet are going. I learn to take care of Ben when he says he isn't doing too well, *one second, two deep breaths, one, two, it'll be okay you'll see.*

On Saturday, the Anglo half of Montreal gathers at Ben's place; it's a world that opens up to me, people whom I know only by name and are less and less clothed as one progresses through the rooms of the house, which were skilfully set up with different lighting and musical styles.

There's Sean's room, the sex room. Aubrey's room, which is the intellectuals' chamber due to the book-cases along the wall. The living room transforms into a dance floor, where softcoresoft mixes tracks with one hand in the air then goes to dance as soon as the transition is arranged. The kitchen's for caffeine and plates of drugs, which lie around left and right, a big mess in front of the closed door of Ben's room, where the objects of value have been hidden.

I follow Ben's advice, who tells me *take x, y, and z.* I nod *yes,* I swallow, I forget everything, but there are photos of me in which my eyes are wide open, so I imagine it went well.

I regain consciousness all the same in the sex room, in the middle of speaking with Sean, who's writing his master's thesis in creative writing — the situation is less carnal than one might have thought it, except that I'm bare naked; I only have my Calvins left, which don't hide much. But Sean isn't gay, and

I really am interested in his writing project; we talk about it for at least four hours—I'm barely exaggerating. At that point, it's eleven in the morning, the DJs have left, so I venture out in search of Ben.

Feeling groggy as fuck, I leave the sex room in my underwear and cross the hall toward the kitchen. In the living room, a tall guy, white toque, shirtless, tattoos in the centre of his chest, tattoos on his neck, red shorts, the kind of guy that I've seen a thousand times online but never in real life, the kind that Bahnhof Zoo shared on their Tumblr before the site was wiped out by censorship, the guy's a lion, the guy's a wolf, my life's a zoo.

We dance a little, we play with our eyes, we flirt as best we can, and we start kissing until we fall onto the sofa. I feel a little bad because I'm like on a date with Ben, but we didn't spend a single second together, so I put it into perspective. The guy is hot enough to die for, and I cum while he strangles me, which I've never experienced before.

(I'm not certain that what I write here really happened. I was too high and it was probably a hallucination. Nonetheless, I had the impression of living out a fantasy in real life. Of course, no one saw this particular guy at the party, I was told that it was possible that he entered through the front because nobody had locked the door. I know that I found myself in a strange place between desire and reality. A place that took me by the throat and didn't let me go.)

It must be four in the afternoon, and Sean and I decide to do more MD, because that's all that's left. It's then that Ben — reappearing all of the sudden without giving any excuse — tells me that because I like techno and I'm drawn to trash, I would be in my element in Berlin. He'll be there this summer staying with Campbell Irvine, his friend who's already played at Berghain. To hear him speak, I imagine that Berghain is a three-storey fetish club where the folks on the second floor piss and poo on the folks on the first, just for the fun of it — and on the second just like on the first everyone's happy.

I implicitly promise to meet up with him during the summer, hoping for more than what he has to give me, then I start to collapse. It's Sunday night; I haven't slept in what seems to me like an eternity. Aubrey and Ben, the lone survivors of the party, talk about going bowling and ordering coke. They don't really know how they'll pay for it, but Aubrey says he might still have some change in his bank account; I let them go and fall asleep in Ben's bed.

That evening, I wait. When Ben finally comes back, Monday morning at six, I hear him make advances on Aubrey, who doesn't react because he's straight. Nonetheless they collapse onto Aubrey's bed — not onto Ben's, where I am, no. I recall swaying between the two rooms while asking myself what I should do: leave, or stay in the hopes of having a moment alone with Ben?

Toward noon, Ben came back into his room where I was twiddling my thumbs. We tried to turn each other on, without success. I held Ben very tight in my arms so that he would stay.

The next day, I bought him forty-five dollars' worth of pizza and fries that we ate while he packed up his things. I was more attached than I wanted to be, undoubtedly due to the drugs that drew out my patience and my emotions.

I left before his taxi for the airport arrived, an untouched pizza in hand. Under the rain, it wasn't going to survive the trip.

FLORIAN
Hasenheide Park, Berlin

At Hasenheide Park, at the hour of sunset, the mosquitoes form a legion and eat the naked bodies of the guys who are penetrating each other between the trees. Freshly disembarked from the plane at Tegel, Emma and I meet up with Ben there to drink a few beers. We're 100 percent tourists; we walk around with big eyes fascinated by what we'd never see this publicly in a Montreal park. Ben has witnessed this spectacle at least a thousand times but agrees to guide us through the space anyway. I learn the code of conduct, the signs to copy and the gestures to avoid; I learn how to open a beer without a bottle opener: in Berlin, you can drink on the street without the police getting on your case.

A part of me is turned on by the spectacle that is performed around us; another is motivated to discover this city I've heard so much about. Advised by Ben, we head toward Ficken 3000 — *ficken*, in German, is the verb *to fuck* — with the half-admitted objective of... fucking, I imagine. I haven't seen Ben since his departure from Montreal, and I'm a bit sad to learn that in Berlin he and his boyfriend decided to be in an exclusive relationship. Sad, but happy for him; he tells me that they've never been stronger as a couple.

To take my mind off it, I very rapidly drink all sorts of alcohol, enough to put me at ease and start talking to everyone. I don't see the time passing. It's five in the morning and a punk-trash German calls me over with two beers and shots of Berliner Luft. The name of the drink means "Berlin air," as if this rather gross minty liqueur could be thought of as a big lungful of fresh air. Not.

We raise a toast to love, and he tells me that his name is Florian. He asks me if I have ten euros, because he would maybe do a little bump of speed so things could take off even more.

My hand in his, he pulls me to the back of the bar, toward the staircase that leads to the dark rooms. I understand immediately that it's there where my initiation will take place. I stop myself and look down. Like in a horror movie when you yell at the

screen for the hero to stay away — *fucking idiot* —
in my head I tell myself: *no, don't go there.* Then
I descend.

My heart blinded, I follow him while we advance
through a thousand different rooms — it's like twice
as big underneath as above, Ficken. I meet his friend,
I forget his name, he gives us some powder, Florian
and I start sucking each other off, he's about to cum,
but stops me, telling me that it'll be more fun back
at his place. Before leaving, he goes into a room
reserved for golden showers because he needs to piss
too badly; we spray each other a bit, laughing.

At that point in the evening, the Berlin air has
gotten the better of me, and I'm not seeing too
straight. I know — because a guy on the street took
photos of us with my phone — that we sucked each
other off on Karl-Marx Strasse while waiting for the
M41. I woke up at Florian's place, anus on fire on
the bathroom floor.

Like with the majority of evenings I spent in Berlin,
I have few memories of this one, but I know it was
trash. Luckily, I still have the photos. It's Emma who
found them in my phone, three weeks later, while
she went through it to see the "pretty photos" that
we took on vacation.

They were very pretty.

EXPERIMENTATION
Berlin, Germany

Sophy and Emma: *You've got nothing to lose, go.*

I decide to take my courage in both hands, to put on my big-boy pants, and to go to this globally "renowned" sex club, one I've heard so much about even before becoming familiar with Berlin. I leave the two girls, shaking a little, and I pass beside Berghain toward the dark path leading to Lab.Oratory, a floor below. Next to the door, a white sign displays the rules of the sex club reserved for men.

PLAY SAFE X DRESS DIRTY
NO DRUGS X NO PERFUME

Even though they say *nein* to no guy — one must remember that Berlin is hyper-phallocentric — I'm stressed from the moment I press on the buzzer and see a sort of pirate with an eyepatch who examines my soul through my eyes and smiles at my ashen appearance. He signals to me to enter and points to the counter where a fifty-year-old gentleman tells me, also with an amused grin, that *you need to put your things in a plastic bag*, a bag that they vacuum-seal to protect the contents. A little zone at the entrance is designated for people to get undressed. Clotheswise, I make do with what I have, seeing as I hadn't antici-pated spending my Friday evening at the Lab: I pull off everything except my white Calvin Klein undies, my Nike TN shoes, and my white Nike socks pulled up right to my ankles, the logo in clear view.

In front of the guys who put on their harnesses and other fetishist accessories, I try to convince myself that I'm game and I enter the dark labyrinthine lab where the music is louder than at Berghain, kind of strange for an environment that isn't dedi-cated to music. But this ultrafamous sex club has understood that an overload of auditory and visual stimuli encourages you to do quite a few things that you wouldn't usually do, a little like being under hypnosis.

Architecturally, the Lab is a sort of circle: if you travel straight you'll end up back where you were at the beginning, but having passed by each of the "themed" rooms, where various fantasies are lived out in turn. First room: a bar with a mezzanine where a guy who's really cute — and embarrassed, like me—chills next to a gang of guys my age, also cute. It's starting off well.

My entrance as a tall beanpole, shoulders up to my ears due to stress, doesn't go unnoticed with the daddies of the place, who cast burning looks at me, while for my part, I eyeball the swimmers / soccer players at the back. I take two beers at the bar, following the theme of the evening (*Friday Fuck 2-4-1*—*Pimp up your weekend*—*Double drinks*), then I enter deeper into the donut.

We'll say it upfront: the rules of the Lab, they're bullshit and no one respects them, except for "no perfume" and "dress dirty," which are too obvious to break. For one, everyone consumes on the sly, which is particularly obvious because of the owl eyes, the smell of poppers, and the restlessness in the air. For two, no one plays safe. I realize this while entering the second room, where a guy tells me that it's a space reserved for bareback. *Not for me, thanks.* I get myself in a hurry into the third room, where a guy's getting fisted by five people in turn.

In the room after that—more industrial, decorated with lots of concrete and steel—a very tall, svelte guy with long brown hair, Swedish type, emerges from the shadows and signals to me to approach. Quite simply I pass between small metal islands designed for having a little intimacy. But before getting to him, a sailor with broken teeth takes me by the hand to lead me off and I escape running, retracing my steps. Even if it's only been about twenty minutes that I've been here, it might be time for me to go.

But as I go back through the bareback room, I see the Swede again in the distance and he prompts me to follow him, which I do, a little stunned by the music and his hair. He takes me far; we pass through among others the pee-pee rooms, where I recognize the golden shower boy from Berghain lying on the floor with his dog collar. We walk to a room that seems absolutely normal, a changing room for men that reminds me of the one that I frequented when I swam at the Olympic Stadium. I lose sight of the Swede and decide to sit down a bit to catch my breath, glad to be alone and to no longer be seen in my white undies.

Just as I'm starting to feel at ease, eight athletes enter, shouting. They're naked and have erections like horses and start whipping each other with wet towels while jostling me with their elbows. I understand that I'm the little nerd who is caught up in a precise fantasy (an exact fantasy of mine, that being said, years before). I struggle to leave, decidedly aroused to see the armpits and pubic hair of these guys who're playing at being athletes from an American high school. I make a break for it because, this evening, I just came to *watch*.

I explore the outside area of the Lab a little, but some old undesirables start to prowl around me. I find a spot to set myself up comfortably in the metal structures that are placed out under the stars, far from them. I note the presence of a guy in a jacket and tie — funny choice, but that can be kinky, no?

He leaves me alone, understanding that that's what I want. Seeing as he seems veeeery nice and he puts me at ease, I decide to approach him, and we chat for a long time while the goblins circle around us. He tells me that he comes from Brazil, that he's already visited Montreal, that he stayed at the Hôtel Gouverneur and that he really liked the Village.

After that, he breaks off and looks me dead in the eyes. In English, he tells me in a solemn tone: *I'm going to give you a piece of advice. At your age, we want everything to change all the time. You think you live for that, but that's also, without you realizing it, what scares you. Once you accept that things settle and you decide to feel good about that slowness, it's going to be simpler for you.*

After, he asks me: *Is it one of your fantasies, to suck off an old guy in work clothes?* I reply no, then I leave.

Inside, having redone the circle, I find the bar again. Disappointed not to see the gang of handsome guys on the mezzanine, I decide to return to the reception, take my vacuum-sealed belongings, and leave. I arrived at quarter to midnight, and it must now be quarter *past* midnight: I consider this an accomplishment. I take the M41, proud, to go tell the girls everything that happened.

BUSINESS OR PLEASURE?
Berlin, Germany

When you meet someone in a club and he asks you *when are you leaving?* there's always a moment of hesitation about whether the question concerns the party or the city. And this question returns night after night. Probably because it's like a curse for the locals: who wants to get attached to a person who's leaving in three weeks?

AMERICAN TOUR
Miami, United States

Vacation in the States with Zach. We land at night
in Miami and get ourselves to a too-cute little apartment, only one bed. At night, I dream that I'm in a
bar with one of my dates of the moment. We devour
each other with our eyes, with our mouths. I'm super
happy because in real life it didn't work out. I take
the opportunity to dance the tango of love for at least
two hours. In the morning, Zach tells me that I tried
to kiss him, pulling him in to spoon. Fuck.

During the week in Miami, there's a single bar where
the gays go, Twist, an immense three-storey affair where
all the rooms blast various genres of music. Which
means Tuesday, Wednesday, Thursday, Friday, and
Saturday, we find ourselves there, no questions asked.
We spend the majority of our time in the pop room,

which is decorated with celebrity portraits everywhere, but we also could have gone into the techno room, with the disoriented ravers, or in the go-go boys space to feast our eyes.

Thursday, in our little cocoon, I scroll on Grindr a little bit frustrated by the imposed limit of fifty visible profiles without a paid subscription. A faceless guy messages me, Zach exclaims that his favourite interactions always start like that. *You never know, it's like a surprise box: either the guy is really ugly and you just have to ghost him, or he's mega-handsome and you just have to suck him off.*

I open the surprise box by agreeing to swap pics on Snapchat — because the guy wants it to be ephemeral; seeing his magnificent penis alone, I get the impression that I haven't found a dud, but it's hard to say since he hasn't sent photos of his face while I have. He promises me that if he finds me to his taste in real life, he'll come talk to me, then it'll be up to me to guess that it's him. Challenge accepted.

Before leaving for Twist, Zach decides to prepare us a drink in his own way: he fills a glass three-quarters with vodka and adds a little quarter of cranberry juice. Like an imbecile, I decide to chug it all; I don't even get to the bar before blacking out.

Well: it wasn't entirely a blackout, but I still managed to pull off a few stupidities. At the bar, I bought six supplementary vodka shooters. The server must have given himself a generous tip while swiping my credit card in the machine, now that I could no longer say no to anything, because the bill came out to $150 US. I lost sight of Zach, who also pulled off quite a few stupidities: between the pop room and the techno room, he vomited in a corner and when he straightened up found himself face to face with the portrait of Britney. *You better work, bitch.*

My biggest stupidity, that was my cruising / searching for drugs in the toilets. Thinking that a bump of coke would wake me up, I went to piss and addressed all the guys who were coming to the urinals to ask them if they'd have any to share. Of course, I also took the opportunity to cruise to the max even if the response was all noes. At a certain moment, a super handsome guy, tall, with the body of a Greek god, arrives next to me and pulls from his pants a sensational penis. My jaw is on the floor. I whip out my pick-up line for him — *You wouldn't know where I could find myself a bump of coke?* The guy instantly seizes me by the neck (after having unfortunately stowed his peen) and tells me that he's the bouncer. He drags me behind him and pitches me outside. I fall to the ground, go to sleep in my vomit.

Luckily, Zach witnesses my humiliating expulsion and takes care of me; he accompanies me back to our apartment.

The next day, misery and shame over what I'd managed to do. Zach doesn't seem too annoyed, but he asks me, smiling slightly, if I heard anything during the night. No, nothing. *At some point, I couldn't find you anymore, but I started cruising your date, y'know, the guy on Grindr. He was real cute, he helped me bring you back here. Afterwards we fucked in the bed while you slept right next to us. But I wasn't stopping to check that you hadn't woken up. You slept like a champion.*

Later in the day, the Grindr dude sent me some photos on Snapchat of me face-down on the sidewalk next to the bar with the caption *Current situation*. The photos don't embarrass me because, by a miracle, I still look cute in my vomit.

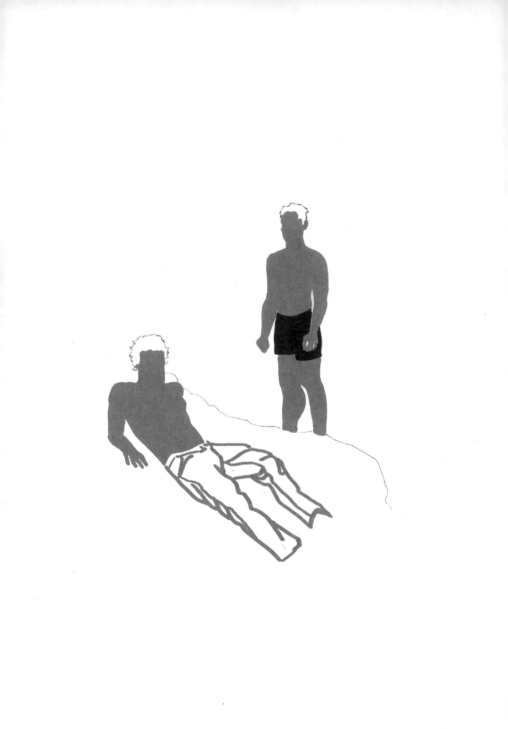

THE RAT CHARMER
Teufelssee, Berlin

In Berlin for the third time. Wherever I go, I have
the impression of chasing after others, of chasing
after myself. The years have taught me that I fall in
love with every person I sleep with — it's systematic,
I'm too sensitive.

I wake up telling myself that I'm going to approach
things differently. I take my things to go to Teufelssee,
text some friends but not lovers, lie down eyes open
in the grass between the nude mature men and the
others, keeping my Speedo on because I'm looking
for peace of mind.

If I wasn't in a depression from too much ecsta and
too many stimuli, I probably would have had fun
with the boys who smoke on my left to niche techno

that I like. I would have gone off to pursue the piper in the legend of the Brothers Grimm, the one in which the little rats are drawn out of the town, swept away by the music. We would have danced, day and night, until we forgot what time means.

But not today. I dive into the lake to take my mind off things, swim my most beautiful crawl to a little artificial island that was created for people to be able to lounge and tan. I arrive at the ladder a little tired, and I run headlong into a blond boy, a young twink who wants to climb up as well; we smile at each other while treading water, water between our teeth.

I gesture to him to go first, no reaction. I move forward a little, he barely moves back, jerks his head backward to indicate a beach farther away, only accessible by swimming. We get there in a few breaststrokes.

When he leaves the water, I discover the thin body of a child who can't be more than fourteen years old. He bears that symmetry that splits adolescents in two, his shoulder blades trace straight parallels the length of his back. He drops his little apple cheeks on a dried tree trunk.

I take my place on the ground, on the sand, rather than sitting next to him. I watch him smile for a long moment until he gets up and points to the forest. I let him take off, then I return to my stuff, swimming breaststrokes.

The boys left, and the music faded out with them.

WOOHOO
Montreal, Quebec

Saturday, a peaceful evening because I have a lot to do: at ten o'clock the next day, I have an appointment for a casting photo with a guy whose work I admire. I meet up with my friends who are organizing a boozy dinner at Sam's place for her birthday; folks are cute lit in neon and in the light of the full moon, which enters through the windows. I don't intend to stay late because I want to seem in good shape in the photos.

I bring Laurence with me after running into her in the street, a friend from school whom I really like. It's the big clash of worlds, the meeting of medieval literature and the underground life—I don't know if I'm ready.

Laurence handles everything well, from the arrival by bike of the dealer who sells me two vials of keta to the immense lines that everyone consumes. I'd warned her of the probable intensity of the evening — but still.

Normal house party composition: to one side, the dance floor with the dinner leftovers on the table, platter of cheese and lots and lots of wine; to the right, the romance room, with bed and New York–style window which overlooks a fire escape with exterior stairs. It's there — and not even on the bed because after all it's a party at Sam's — that people devour each other.

I offer myself up to everyone, I catch up with those whom I haven't seen in a long time while offering lines, and I reconnect with others I saw yesterday doing the same thing — let's keep it real, there's always a moment when I no longer know what to say, and I break the silence by introducing my good friend Kate (a code name for ketamine).

Kate is really partying it up this evening, not too strong but a little psychedelic, she put on her pretty acid dress to seduce us. And the full moon brings out the Cancer in us (that's the coke); everything works for the better.

The lights of the kitchen sparkle.

I eat a little cheese.

In the latest news, Laurence is doing well. I spot her with a little boy. A newcomer who seems nice. I leave them in peace for their one-on-one on the metal stairs.

In the living room, the party goes around in circles. Opi introduces us to their new discovery of the moment: the song "Woohoo" by HOSH. There's something circular in the progression of the tune and right away it's a hit. We play it enough times to forget when the song ends and when it begins.

People dance alone, then in groups. It's extremely loud in the living room with wine-stained smiles. Behind us, neon pulses calmly to the beat, a rhythm a little slower than that of my heart.

When we finally decide to stop the tune, it's light outside. Laurence has been gone for quite some time — with or without her boy, I don't know. Outside, marathon runners exercise and families head to brunch.

It's not too late for my photo session, but my goblin look says otherwise.

GOBLINS
Berlin, Germany

The rule is: past eight in the morning in a rave that drags on and on, when it seems like everyone around you is a goblin, the thing is — you are one as well.

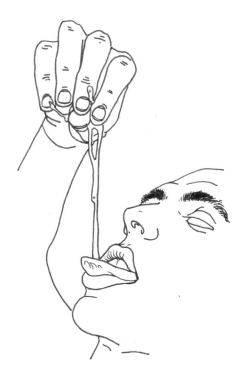

X-MEN
Berlin, Germany

Cocktail is on fire under the sun and the techno.
I've never seen so many gays assembled without it
ending in a big squabble. The muscles get along with
the nerds. The dedicated ravers get along with the
tourists. How unlikely.

Something's going to blow.

My friend Édu is at the centre of the mass, a drop
in the ocean of wriggling sweat; I would love to
offer him a bump of keta, but that would take too
much effort. I abandon that idea and decide to serve
myself, alone, on a little leather couch that's placed
at the back of the room, so far away that security
won't bother to come kick me out if they catch me
in flagrante delicto.

Fanny pack. Hand in the bag, I take what I need: big key for our Neukölln apartment, cracked phone, some cards, fifty-euro bill because I decide to do a line in the end—fifties are less dirty than other bills, at least I dare to believe it. Exhale, to clear the nose. Inhale.

I raise my head to see whether what I'm currently doing is scandalous. It is. Eight hundred thousand ravers sway in front of me, starved junkies who search with their eyes for their junk—keta, it's like a pack of gum: as soon as you open it, everyone holds out their hand. Avoid eye contact at any price.

A German as handsome as Fassbender stares at me a few metres ahead. I would have liked to lower my head, but I wasn't able to. That's only happened to me a few times in my life, seeing someone in the distance and knowing that we're made for each other. Like two lovers drawn together.

With the mix of sun, drugs, and all the rest, it seems to me like we've known each other forever; we look at each other for such a long time that everything is said. Except that's not true, and he advances toward me. I'm a bit scared, but on my couch with the drugs and my things strewn about, my reaction time is pretty much nil: I can't do anything before he gets to me and extends his hand. *Gabriel?*

I freeze for a second. Grindr? Or Tinder? I doubt it: Tinder is an app much too slow for the rhythm of Berlin and everyone ends up flushing it. If not, it must be that he comes from Montreal and I already met him; the more I think about it the likelier that seems: this guy, though I don't really know why, makes me think of Durocher, of the shadowy corners way in the back.

I don't want to miss the chance that it works out between us, so I play the game by giving the most awkward *hey!* of my life, followed by the most banal question of all time: *How long have you been here?*

In Berlin or at Cocktail?

Euh, both?

He laughs a bit.

I was born in Germany. Just got here.

Fuck. That eliminates the possibility of Montreal. But in the past few years, I've slept with more people than I could list; I thus don't exclude the possibility that we spent time together, even that we fucked. At a party, I once introduced myself to a guy, in flirting mode and everything, whom I had actually dated years before. The guy hadn't made the connection either. We had the time to fall back in love before the friend he was with reminded us that we'd dated and that it ended badly.

Back to my handsome Fassbender. I take the initiative of inviting him to the bar so we can talk, but secretly, I just want us to go into the dark rooms. He replies tit for tat: *But what about Édu?* I freeze big time. *He's gonna be fine,* I reply.

Mister Muscles leads the way, pushing everyone aside and protecting me; charming. As though he read my thoughts, he completely avoids going to the bar and heads down into the dark rooms, then settles on a little wooden bench, not uncomfortable, in the dark.

The sex is better than the random one-night stands that I had in the preceding weeks, which makes me think more and more that we already slept together. In fact, the guy is hyper-tactile and finds all my sweet spots without me having to show them to him. I cum quickly, played like a violin (sorry for the corny expression).

Going back up to the dance floor, Fassbender gives me a beautiful showy little smile, looking pleased with himself. He says to me *See you later?* but I have no hope. In the back of my mind, I try again to remember our first encounter. He must have come to Montreal before and I forgot to ask him about it.

Or else I slept with an X-Man.

SELFIE
Berghain / Panorama Bar

At Berghain, the mirrors were pulled off the walls, probably to discourage anyone from seeing themselves after eighteen hours of partying, eye bags, cross-eyed, grey-faced from hunger, the whites of their eyes reddened by lack of sleep.

When I use the camera of my phone to look at myself, to make sure that everything's still there, I'm always scared of the same thing: of seeing eye bags that won't leave, premature wrinkles that have gotten the better of me, as though they're saying *you went too far. Now, it's irreversible.*

POOL PARTY
Berlin, Germany

I enter Pornceptual, and I hear in the distance a remixed version of "Swim" by Nicolas Jaar. It fits with my look of the moment because to meet the requirements of the party and reduce my entry fee according to my level of "undress," I decided to go in a Speedo and swimming goggles.

It also fits because for ten years, swimming organized my life. It was what occupied the majority of my free time outside of school, what secured me a group of friends, what forced me to get myself up Saturday mornings at six to voluntarily pitch myself into a pool of cold water.

So while I wade through the halls of Pornceptual, I think I'm really serving swimmer's realness.

It's the eighth evening in a row that I'm spending with Édu, but we never go back home together after the party. I could spend half an hour enumerating all the profanities that cross my mind, so much does this annoy me, but I'm more proactive than that in life and I try to bring out my A game so that this evening, please please please, it will work and we'll break the curse that's been cast on us.

Anyway, Édu nods *hey* at me and I decide to follow him below, damn charmer.

We go down toward the room decorated as a gym locker, just next to the golden shower room, and it reminds me again of the years at the swimming club. With the big techno beat that swallows all other noise, it's impossible for me to tell Édu that at the pool of my adolescence, to get "pissed on" was a threat. You pass me on the left doing the breaststroke while I'm in the middle of doing two hundred metres of cooldown? The next time that I pass you, I'm going to piss on you.

It could also go further. The coach picked you to demonstrate a dive? Beware the hot water that you're going to swallow the next time I swim in front of you. The whole gang is seeing red because you didn't want to date Camille, the girl who met the national standard in the crawl? Watch out, because we're opening the jets.

It was a common thing to threaten others with one's piss.

Of course, at Pornceptual, people piss merrily in each other's mouths. I wouldn't even cry if Édu took me by the arm to bring me into that particular dark room; I'd have a little smile at the corner of my mouth. But all he does is direct me toward one of the rooms designated for dancing. Booooring.

The crowd sweats so much that the air is compact and beads drop from the ceiling directly into our mouths. It's the kind of humidity that completely destroyed a roll of line that we kept in the men's changing room at the pool even though it was infested with mould. I had to circumvent it to go in the showers, except I never really had to do it because I avoided the showers like an alcoholic avoids going to boozy dinners.

To my great happiness, Édu ends up turning to me — to touch my dick — and brings me onto an old wooden bench where we plunge into each other. Our bodies are completely aqueous, so much so that I no longer really know what's mine and what's his. My tongue is in its favoured element, apparently, because it escapes his mouth to start licking everything, from top to bottom, from left to right, from the inside outward.

An ease that I didn't have at sixteen years old, when I found myself in a hotel room with another swimmer during team championships. A dream: two gays, one assumed, one not, alone for a whole night; you'd think that the coach had planned the thing. In fact, it was quite the opposite. I will always remember my friend's devastated expression as he explained to me that he got pissed on in the showers because he'd supposedly watched one of the boys wash himself. But he hadn't watched, because drawing attention to oneself by showing desire for others, that was the last thing that a young gay wanted at the time.

I no longer know if I was capable of finding the right things to say. Maybe I simply rested my head on his shoulder, thinking that we were good, far from the showers and the homophobia of the others.

Ten years later, I emerge from my osmosis with Édu, flowing with all my joy; we celebrate the fact of having found each other again in this rathole. Finally leaving Pornceptual *together*, we get on our bikes, and I think about nothing while pedalling toward my little Neukölln apartment. Emma is in Prague for the weekend.

Except that Édu wavers behind me, ignores me by playing on his phone. Time stops and I understand that I got carried away for nothing. *Things are complicated for me right now. It's nothing against you, obviously.*

My face lowers toward the ground, defeated.

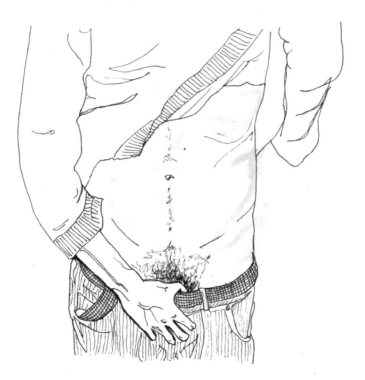

GAY FALLS
Chutes Sainte-Marguerite, Sainte-Adèle

My stepdad came back, all proud, from his little excursion to catch Wi-Fi outside the chalet: *It's at Exit 69!* All he'd had to do was type *Gay falls* into Google to find an article on the famous police raid of 2017, supposedly directed against nudity. He looked at Jake and me with a million-dollar smile: *I wonder what you're going to do over there!*

We pack two or three things, beer above all, and my mom has the kindness to drive us right to Sainte-Adèle. *Be careful; yes, yes, maman.*

We meet up with Vincent and the others at the local snack bar, where the atmosphere is already gay due to the shirtless tanned muscular guys who order themselves hot dogs. We buy even more beer and chips. I transport two packets of Doritos under my armpits while we climb down the mountain to get to the falls; the Bold BBQ one is lost when I jump from one rock to the other, and the Spicy Roulette one is taken away on the current when I cross the river to get to the enchanted forest, the main spot.

Right away we run into Laurent and his new boyfriend, who are wearing mini Speedos. I immediately note that Laurent is cupping his hands under his ass. *I don't want to lose my loads!* he says while jumping into the water.

His "loads," that's the sperm of the guys that he just fucked on the other bank, between the pine trees.

I laugh — not yet knowing that his remark would become my party joke for the coming months — then I look again at his new boyfriend to see if it bothers him that Laurent got himself inseminated by the dudes of the other bank. I consider myself prudish for these thoughts.

In the distance, Pat dances with his mid-length hair and his abs. We greet each other and talk about school, work, as per usual; I feel that our conversation avoids the point. I ask him who he's dating these days; he points to his boyfriend and another guy: *Those two are having a little summer fling. For me, it's him.* Points to another guy.

I turn toward Vincent: *Seems like it's shiny and cute, in the forest. We'll go see?*

Not difficult to convince him; he gambols in front of me like a little white stag ready to rejoin the enchanted creatures. The harvest is good, we immediately spot ogres with their clubs at the edge of the woods. I avert my eyes from them. Farther in, little fairies suck off other little fairies. Snow White's seven dwarfs, in a circle, watch each other while touching themselves.

I leave Vincent at a bend, and I turn back toward the falls with a very specific plan in mind: I run into Jacob, whom I try to daze; it doesn't work, to my great displeasure. I try again fifteen minutes later, while Laurent, not far, seems really pleased and satisfied, the little fucker, with the success that he's had today.

I sit down on the little rock and look around me. Everyone is loaded: Laurent, Vincent, Pat and his friends... I remake the connections between them in my head, to observe that they've found new ways to inter-date.

Enough is enough. I take Jacob by the hand, and I position him behind me. We retrace the path backwards, then stop a few metres away from a group of wolves accompanied by Little Red Riding Hood. I drop my underwear and tell him *we're done beating around the bush!*

A little later — not much later, to be honest —
I come back to the falls, hands and knees covered
in earth, and shove Doritos into my mouth.

The way back was easier than the way there: we had
fewer things to transport. Just my load, which I easily
clenched in my ass while crossing the river.

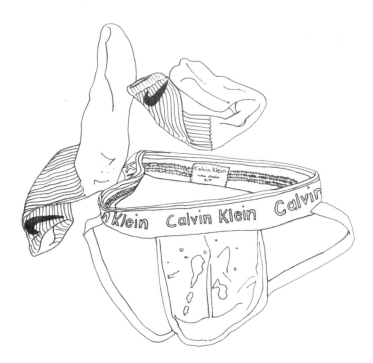

DESCRIPTION
Berlin, Germany

This morning, in the rat's nest that is this after-party, people dance with a certain enthusiasm, smiles on their faces, unbalanced for lack of sleep, eyes shining, cells burnt but glad to be so — everything that seems necessary to survive.

The masc-for-mascs endure despite the lack of protein. The gym's far away, muscles say. Sitting in my corner, I watch them thriving, not displeased with the spectacle that's offered to me — a real pleas ure for the eyes — not afraid to be a voyeur because here everyone is.

For the big Pride weekend, the mascs have trimmed their beards and accompany themselves with big fans that they sweep merrily in front of their faces.

It's also the mascs who have to undergo the ordeal of putting the bottle of g in their ass, with a condom around it. They take a taxi from the house to avoid having to walk too much, but still: bottle in the ass during the hour-long wait before entering, bottle in the ass when the bouncer asks them how many they are in their group, bottle in the ass and ill at ease while they're felt up at the entrance by a madame who wouldn't in any case have the right to do an anal search. For that, I owe them one: it's they who will refill the life-saving millilitres for me when no other drug will succeed in activating my tired body.

Next to them, not very far, between the tourists and the gorillas, the thirty-somethings who work in fashion, branded by their brands, haughty in their beauty, and protected by the posh folks who surround them. I recognize them because they're always here — rats like the others — decked out to buy and sell: they come to consume young boys who will later on become fashion themselves.

Obviously, they avoid black — colours are in fashion and colours are arrogant, a hard stance that pays off in this rave where everyone's alike: they're different, people notice them. I already slept with one of them. That was orchestrated via Instagram, and all that I have left of that affair is a bunch of likes on my photos. We never spoke to each other again.

Despite everything, I follow him with my gaze, no more interested in him than in the others, but as

I watch him, I see there's something pleasant in following the romances of the moment, from the cruise on the dance floor to the toilets where people line up to moan. Contrary to all the other rats, the fashion thirty-somethings put a third layer of foundation under their eyes, to hide the bags that take over their faces and, truly, that works: one would believe them to be the freshest in the place.

The music is nothing special. It's loud enough to boost the dancers' heart rates, but unremarkable enough for us to be focused on the guys that surround us. On the other hand, the techno lighting is a success, the space opens and closes before our eyes by the magic of light; for a moment, one might believe oneself to be in a Gothic cathedral, in part because of the spots that give the impression of having passed through a stained-glass window, but mostly because I took too many drugs and my mind is turning medieval.

Between the apparently watertight groups, a no man's land is created. My fashion guy approaches one of the masc-for-mascs, a handsome Tristan of indeterminate age, without his Iseult. I have the feeling they'll know love and death; I stop being interested in the others to concentrate on them.

Normally, cruising happens naturally because you seduce someone who's more or less similar to you, but here, I see it, they flounder, with no remaining common language, what one does intimidates the other. Finally it's settled by the most universal question of all time: *Should we go do a bump in the toilets?*

The line is long when one has nothing to say, french-ing allows the whole thing to be accelerated, but still, it's peak hour, all the rats think of their Gruyère, salivating, they would've had to make a move an hour earlier. The lovers hear, jealous, the passionate cries of the others who got to it in advance, it turns them on just like it turns me on.

I could give long descriptions of the hair of one of the men against the other's body, of the coloured shirt against the absence of a shirt, of muscles against the unmotivated beginning of a training regimen, of trendy glasses that sit between devouring eyes, except everyone is just frustrated with waiting, again. It's like that every weekend; the boss of the place should think about adding more stalls. The fashion guy and his masc-for-masc could fuck and do a bump in the dark rooms, but that seems too trash for them.

And things eventually advance. Unblock. The guys choose a stall, don't even prepare a line, letting out the clutch on what's important. I wait barely two more minutes to place myself in the adjacent stall, where I listen to them moan, yeah. But bored, I decide to cut myself too-big lines to kill the time.

KATER BLAU
Berlin, Germany

Monday morning hangover. A few hours before my departure. A month and a half spent dating and networking, encounters that give the impression that they'll last.

I've just said my goodbyes to Berghain, and I decide to meet up with Edu, who isn't too far away, in a very different club: if at Berghain one must be dressed in black and love chains and BDSM gear, at Kater Blau one must love colours, mismatched clothes, and cheery music. Except that at the moment of meeting up with Édu, I have a bad bout of depression and zombie eyes, and my body is smudged with grime and filth. It's the fact of leaving that's making me this down, probably.

A drag queen placed in front of the door systematically rejects everyone. It's true that people are badly dressed, but the two hippies in front of me seem to correspond exactly to the place's aesthetic. I progress through the line too brain-dead to ask myself if I fit in or not.

After the particularly scathing rejection of the hippies — *You should pay someone to give you a lesson in styling* — it's my turn. I move forward under the neon lights. I offer myself to her absolute judgement. Taking her sweet time to scrutinize me, from my black shoes in tatters to my eye bags, she then gives her response.

Nein.

I've never done this before — and I'll never do it again — but I decide to plead my case: I explain to her that it's the last opportunity for me to see a fleeting love; if she separates us, it's done for good. I lay it on thick, I unpack for her a tale that's worthy of the film *The Notebook*.

She listens to my speech and answers me, simply:

You know what?

I. Hate. Love.

And furthermore, she says, *you know why you're not allowed in?* She takes me by the arm: *because of this.*

She places her finger on the Berghain stamp that marks my wrist. *You made an effort to dress like them, so make one to dress like us.*

I take a taxi, sixty euros to go change. On the way there, I explain the situation to the driver, who tells me I should have expected as much: Kater Blau has a reputation to uphold. I go up to the apartment, pick up clothes left and right—I have nothing colourful in my wardrobe. (Sportswear flash and colours weren't yet in fashion, or if they were, I wasn't up to speed.) I choose a dark blue shirt. Blue, that counts as a colour, no?

The driver looks me up and down: *Are you crazy? Go put on colours; she warned you.*

I end up putting on a shirt that Florian gave me when I arrived in Berlin. A Neapolitan ice cream–style shirt that I was going to toss but that I decided to keep out of affection.

I've never looked so bad in my entire life. But that permitted me to spend a part of the night at Kater Blau, that club that I nonetheless hate.

NOTHING BREAKS LIKE A HEART
Montreal, Quebec

Returning from Les Printemps du MAC, an event
which we agreed to attend so we could play club kids,
JF and I rush to meet our Uber who swears he's in
front of the event venue (at New City Gas). In the
end, he is three hundred metres east next to a ditch
on the side of the highway.

Of course, if the driver is this disoriented, it's because
he's high, and we sense that it's going to be a big
party as soon as we get into the car. He confesses to
us that his thing at the moment, when he's alone, is
listening to the same song on a loop *ad vitam aeter-*
nam: "Nothing Breaks Like a Heart" by Miley Cyrus.

JF, in the backseat, shouts, HEY, THAT'S MY TUNE!

The volume at max: without any musical ambition at all, we yell *this world can hurt you* because we feel it so much; I raise my arms in the air, we the disappointed lovers belt out the chorus, half-sad, half-laughing, because the moment is frankly ridiculous.

Like in the clip, we think we're in a manhunt / club-kid hunt; we're pursued for having committed the most dangerous crimes, and I, like a chump, I don't realize that we're rolling along at 140 km/h. JF taps me on the shoulder, eyes wide, as though saying *what the fuck.*

It really does seem like nothing, oh nothing can save us at this point.

Despite everything, when the tune starts again, I shout my head off, I yell because Printemps was really nice photo-wise and I took advantage of my fifteen minutes of glory during which I had the impression of being followed by the paparazzi (who were there primarily for the participants of *Occupation Double Grèce*, I admit) but still, on the flirting front, it seems to me that I didn't get as much eye contact as all that, even though I was dressed to the nines. The lyrics possibly teasing me, I'm wondering: did we leave them cold as ice?

At the end of the third repetition of the tune, the car stops in front of JF's apartment; he gets out, and I understand what's going to happen: I will be alone in the taxi with the driver, who is no longer in his right mind, for at least twenty minutes—that's the time it'll take us to get to my place in Outremont.

He turns himself around: *again?* I take my courage in both hands, nod *yes*, and after the fifteen seconds of intro I yell my love to Miley louder than ever.

I dance like the devil while the driver holds out his fist-microphone. I'm the perfect singer for this tune; I forget that we're one swerve from smashing into a utility pole or a street lamp across from a Couche-Tard.

I decide to not half-ass things. If my personal hell is to listen to "Nothing Breaks Like a Heart" a hundred times in a row, I'm here for it.

GHB
Berghain / Panorama Bar

The fourth time that I'm back in Berlin, things have changed. While I wait impatiently to leave again, I spend my time on the phone with people from Montreal. Luckily Sophy, Emma, and Sam are with me, because I don't know what I would have done without them.

My mind is elsewhere, but that doesn't prevent me from going to Berghain, where I disappear among the twinks. This evening is special because it's the first time that Sophy is entering this frankly questionable place.

I hold her tight in my arms. *We're probably going to spend the next fourteen hours here, we shouldn't lose each other.* And I'm saying that in every sense: lose sight of each other, yes, but above all lose ourselves in the drugs and the knockout techno beat that reigns everywhere. Sophy doesn't seem scared — it's me who's exaggerating, as is my habit.

We decide to explore the place under the effects of ketamine, because disorientation contributes to the intrigue of this space. We go to the toilets in the hall, at the back on the right, and we position ourselves behind Oscar; his twin brother, Daniel the illustrator; and Stina, whom I'd kissed before even though I rarely kiss girls. That time, she told me with a magnificent smile that *she will never forget me*. We greet the gang, Stina clicks with Sophy — a more likely match than the couple that she and I would have made — and we wait patiently to enter the stall as a group.

Inside, it's a real competition: we're looking to crown the one who can do the most imposing lines. Oscar, a regular of the place, sets the bar high when he cuts himself one that's relatively thin, but particularly long. Daniel, who arrived earlier than everyone else and who is thus ahead consumption-wise, does one better. Stina and Sophy look at each other, a little terrified, but play the game. I don't know what comes over me: I decide to show off as though my honour depended on it, and I make a line that's quite simply unreasonable and that strikes me all at once, as if I'd been stunned by a lance in a knightly tourney.

Just to worsen our state, Oscar and Dan withdraw from their fanny packs some vials of GHB, which they start to measure out. Round 2. I overdo it again, taking more than necessary; I can no longer manage to stand up straight, but I take even more. At the same time, I hear Sophy crying. I turn toward her: her line — much too big for ten o'clock on a Sunday morning — completely burned the inside of her nose; it wells up to her eyes, which puff up a bit and become red. Her tears are unstoppable, they flow, they flow — got to go fetch water at the first-floor bar to rinse, drink, do something, I don't know what.

Except that at this point, it's almost impossible for me to put one foot in front of the other. My life is a Godard film, and I play the role of the voice-over, not capable of so much as imposing myself, and Sophy cries; we're not out of the woods. We decide to advance, the Oscars and Daniels appear in double in front of me, and I decide to follow their trail because it's the only thing I can do; I can go forth nowhere they haven't gone first; it's hard to explain it but that's how it is.

Sophy, victorious, takes me by the arm and shows me a bench in the middle of the room. Afterwards, I realized that we were next to the statue of a Greek god with his head cut off, only twenty metres from the stall from which we'd emerged, on the first floor, but our journey had seemed to me like a crossing of the oceans. We sit.

I think a good forty-five minutes pass while we hold each other at close quarters, for fear of falling. The

effect of the keta and the g—a mix I don't recom-
mend to anyone—eventually fades, and the damn
narration of my life disappears; I regain consciousness
minute by minute. In my pocket, the vibration of
my cell brings me back to earth a little. I recognize
Jacob's name, but I'm not in good enough shape to
respond.

The moment I stow my phone in my pocket, I'm
snatched up by a little tornado that kisses me,
directly before Sophy's astonished eyes. On me is
Florian and his mohawk, goblin-like, happy to see
me. Me, too, I'm happy-happy, even if I know that it
complicates my life to stumble across a former lover.

He asks right away if we have some speed or something
more prized to share; we go up to the second floor. Our
entry onto the dance floor is spectacular; we take the
time to make the most of it. Afterwards, we go to the
toilets, where a three-hour line awaits us. *I know a
shortcut*, says Florian. We follow him into the dark
rooms.

We position ourselves next to a guy costumed as a
police officer with his baton held up, who doesn't
seem to be complaining about our arrival. We unpack
our things, even take the risk of using our phones like
flashlights in a less occupied corner of the room to
see where we're putting our keys. I no longer know
how I feel about being with Florian, two years after
our encounter. I try to catch up with him, but the
questions that I throw out into the air don't lead to

any conversations because he's mainly interested in the drugs we're giving him.

When we leave the dark rooms, he nonetheless takes me by the arm, tells me that he's happy to see me, that it's been a while. Sophy stays with me while I follow Florian everywhere like a little bunny, though I'm annoyed by the lack of attention and my own desire to please. We go up to the third floor, to the mezzanine that overlooks Panorama. Florian introduces me to his Brazilian friends, and it's at that very moment that I know it's over. Faced with those who have just come up, people with whom he has real connections, I don't see how I can be alone with him.

I decide to take the bull by the horns. While he talks to a Brazilian—a really hot girl, according to Sophy—I manage to find Oscar again and ask him for—*it's really an emergency I promise you I'll pay you back*—three vials of magic elixir that I brandish proudly in front of Florian and Sophy. Luckily, no one can resist my offer, and our little trio returns to the cool kids' toilets below, on the Panorama level.

We measure out quantities of g that are much too large, except for Sophy, who's wise; I fear that this obliges her to be the "designated driver" of the evening. We decide to mix everything with keta. Recovered from the incident at the beginning of the evening, Sophy says that she is *able to take some* (she won't be driving anything much in any case). She's tracing lines on my phone when a call from Jacob causes a photo of his face to pop up on the screen. Too bad, I don't manage to cut the lines in time to take the call.

The next minutes become hours in my head, hours that we spend on the dance floor of Berghain in the gay section just next to the dark rooms. Florian and I, we dance pressed together, and normally I would have had the impression (because of the keta) that we were in the process of intertwining into the other, but that doesn't happen. I just feel like I'm falling; each new sample added to the music provokes the same effect: I'm falling, I don't really know what it is I'm doing, everything is losing its meaning.

When the effect of the k and g dissipates, Florian looks at us with eyes keen to know if we have more; I'd just bummed three vials from Oscar and don't want to annoy him again. I keep my eyes lowered while Sophy explains that she's going to meet back up with Charlotte. It's three in the morning, and we're between two highs — even the idea of getting involved in another round tempts no one. I squeeze Sophy in my arms and tell myself she's going to get back okay. When I turn back around, Florian is gone.

I no longer know if I looked for him for a little bit or if I gave up right away. I know that I went around in circles to find Daniel; his twin, Oscar; Stina, saying my goodbyes to Berghain at the same time. Less than fifteen minutes after Sophy's departure, I was in a taxi. I saw Florian dancing alone, absent-minded, before I left for good.

The thing is with Berlin, it's that people are more interested in doing drugs than in building relationships. You meet people left and right, partners in crime, but there's always the risk of it stopping there.

Upon my return from Berghain, I film myself under the shower pissing on myself, a declaration of love that I send to Jacob.

(2017–2019)

NOTE

The dealer's words on page 71 are borrowed freely from the play *Dans la solitude des champs de coton* (*In the Solitude of the Cotton Fields*) by Bernard-Marie Koltès (trans. Elina Taillon).

ACKNOWLEDGEMENTS

My deep thanks to Jeanne Simoneau, first reader of *Scenes from the Underground*, whose precious artistic and editorial advice permitted me to give form to this project, as well as give me the confidence necessary to share it. Jeanne, you rock.

To Pierre-Luc, prime discussion partner who was able to elevate *Scenes* to what it is now. Thank you for your generosity.

To the goblins with whom I've explored the corridors of the underground: Samuelle, Emma, Sophy, Alej, Max, JF, Vincent, Ben, Florian, Bert, Édu, Mika, Anton, Rouz, Phil, Valentin, Oli, Aubrey, Sean, Manue, Zach, Marie, Marc, Ayisha, Bobby, Oscar, Lili, Mathieu, Clément, Thomas, Dillon, Marine, Jacqui, Anas, Camille, Leticia, Sam, Laurence, Opi, Laurent, Pat, Stina, and Daniel.

To Jacob, to whom the *Scenes* were written as a love letter meant to impress.

—Gabriel Cholette

TRANSLATOR ACKNOWLEDGEMENTS

I would like to thank Gabriel for the immensely helpful guidance as I undertook my first translation project. You answered my most hair-splitting questions with patience and good humour, and being able to consult the author about the nuances of a text was a particular treat.

Thanks as well to Joshua Greenspon for improving my work with excellent editorial sense, for welcoming me at Arachnide from the start, and for all the cheer and enthusiasm. Working with you is a joy.

Thank you to Karim for your unwavering support and for listening to my tangents on the subject of translation.

And thanks, of course, to Namya for your keen interest in my literary endeavours and for always wanting to know how *Scenes from the Underground* was coming along.

—Elina Taillon

©JustineLatour

GABRIEL CHOLETTE (@gab.cho) scours the New York, Berlin, and Montreal underground scenes for literary material, which he writes on using the codes of Instagram. He has a PhD in medieval French literature.

Montreal artist JACOB PYNE (@cumpug) explores themes of sexual identity, relationships, and anonymous sex from a queer perspective. His intimate and erotically charged scenes are inspired by his personal experiences and desires.

ELINA TAILLON is a queer, neurodiverse writer, MFA candidate in the University of British Columbia's Creative Writing program, and the former managing editor at PRISM *international* magazine. She also holds a master's degree in French literature from the University of Toronto. She has published book reviews in PRISM and *Young Adulting*, prose in *Déraciné* and *filling Station*, and poetry in CV2 and *The /tɛmz/ Review*. This is her first translation for Arachnide.